# Rip it! Tip it!

Written by Tina Pietron

**Collins**

Meg pops a hat on.

Rod has a red hat.

Ram into the rocks.

Ken hits and taps.

Rip the rocks up.

Rick digs a pit.

It tips on top.

It is red hot.

Ron hops up on it.

10

It sets it on top.

It gets the muck.

It is a din!

hum

# After reading

**Letters and Sounds:** Phase 2

**Word count:** 52

**Focus phonemes:** /g/ /o/ /c/ /k/ ck /e/ /u/ /r/ /h/

**Common exception words:** has, into, the, is, and

**Curriculum links:** Understanding the world

**Early learning goals:** Reading: read and understand simple sentences; use phonic knowledge to decode regular words and read them aloud accurately; read some common irregular words

## Developing fluency

- Your child may enjoy hearing you read the book.
- You could each choose which pages to read. Check your child does not miss reading the label on page 13.

## Phonic practice

- Turn to pages 4 and 5. Point to **rocks** and **Ken**. Ask your child to point to the letters in each word that make the /k/ sound. (**ck** and **K**)
- Turn to page 12 and ask your child to find the word with the /ck/ sound. (*muck*)
- Look at the "I spy sounds" pages (14 and 15). Point to the /h/ and then the helicopter and say: I spy a /h/ in helicopter. Take turns to point to and name a word that contains the /h/ sound. (e.g. *hot, house, hat, helmet, hammer, hit, hills, hole*)

## Extending vocabulary

- Turn to pages 12 and 13 and ask your child to make the **hum** sound of the truck.
- Turn to pages 4 and 5 and ask what the sounds might be for this page. Can your child think of other words for loud noises? (e.g. *bang, crash*)